Weebies Family Fireworks Night English Language

English Language British Full Colour

Written by

Alastair R Agutter

ALL RIGHTS RESERVED

ILLUSTRATED COVER:
By Alastair R Agutter

Children's Weebies Family

ORIGINAL CHARACTERS CREATED
By Alastair R Agutter

ORIGINAL ARTWORK AND ILLUSTRATIONS
By Alastair R Agutter

www.alastairagutter.com

Children's Weebies Characters Copyright 2005 to 2014

Copyright © Paperback First Edition 2014

PUBLISHED BY

Create Space Independent Publishing
An Amazon Group Company

First Edition Published: 4th November 2014

ISBN-13: 978-1503140110

ISBN-10: 1503140113

ALL RIGHTS RESERVED

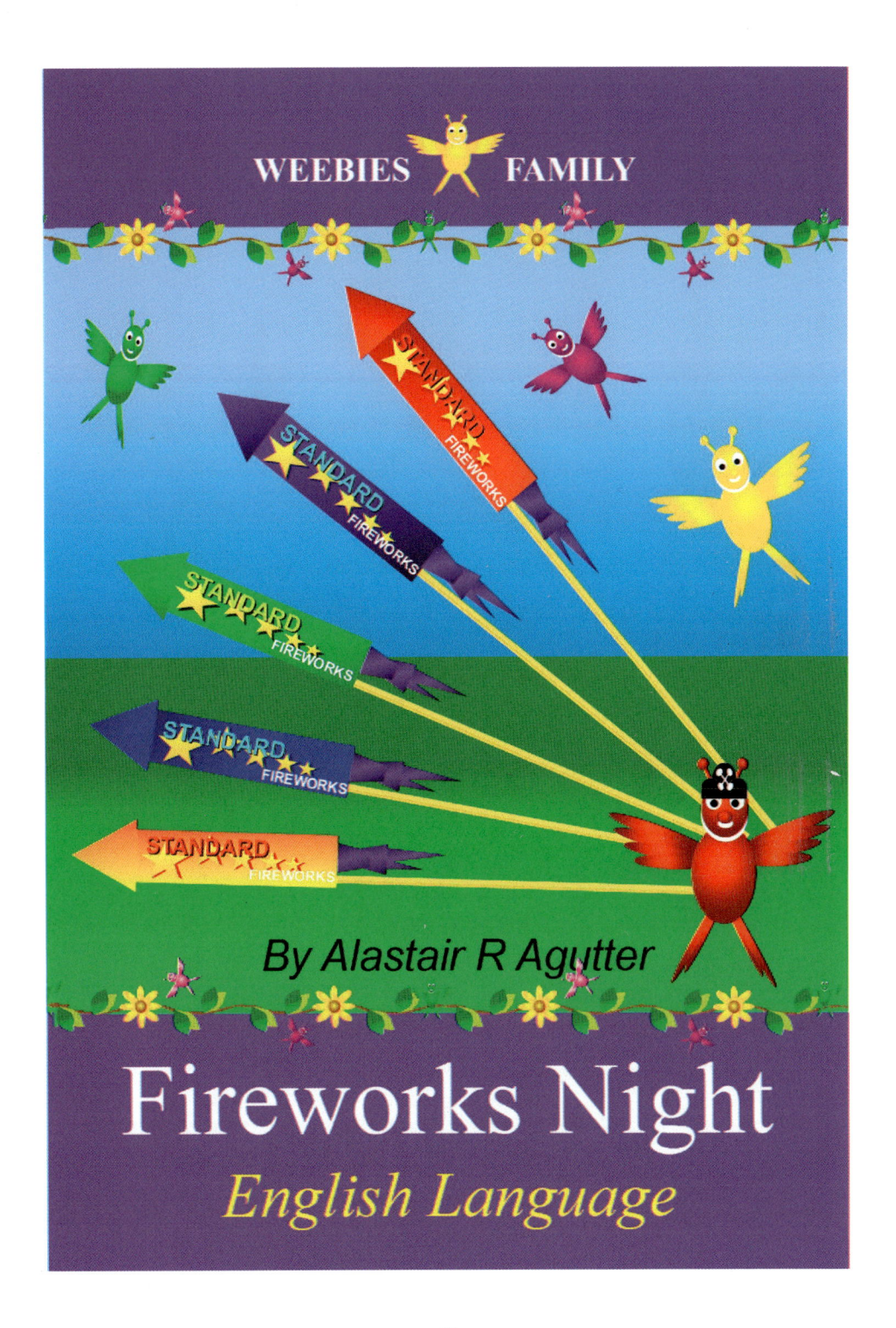

Fireworks Night
English Language

By Alastair R Agutter

WEEBIES FAMILY

Children's Weebies Characters

Veronica Twizzle Top

Hello Hello Hello

Honey

Morgan the Pirate

Grumpy Gammy

Busy Billy

Great Aunt Andorra

Created By Alastair R Agutter

Weebies Say Hello

Hello and Welcome,

To the 'Weebies Family Fireworks Night Book' is part of the Children's Weebies series.

Here at Weebies we are always very busy and learning of new things as we have lots of fun.

In this book 'Weebies Fireworks Night' we tell you about traditions and things a family do together.

Each short story tells you about the activities and events the Weebies Family get up to for their Firework Night.

If you like making pictures there are lots in this book you can copy and draw to make up your own Weebies stories.

Weebies are always kind and very busy bringing 'Sunshine' into our world.

Happy Weebies Fun!

WEEBIES FAMILY

Alastair R Agutter

Fireworks Night

The Weebies Family Plan Fireworks Night

It was a very special day today for the Weebies Family and more so for the Children Morgan, Billy and Honey.

The day had finally arrived where it was **'Fireworks Night'** a special event that the Weebies Children really liked a lot.

The Weebies Children were flying around all very excited today and in the distance they could see **'Great Aunt Andorra'** arriving, to tell the Weebies Children more stories and tales.

'Great Aunt Andorra' was loved by the Weebies Children, as she could make magic to lighten up their World.

The Weebies Children's Dad **'Hello Hello Hello'** started laughing as he saw **'Great Aunt Andorra'** arriving on a broomstick.

WEEBIES FAMILY

Fireworks Night

Great Aunt Andorra Arrives For Fireworks Night

'**Great Aunt Andorra**' finally arrived and all the Weebies Family gathered together to make plans for the day a head.

'**Great Aunt Andorra**' was going to help the Weebies Children's Mummy, '**Veronica Twizzle Top**' and '**Honey Weebie**' make and get ready the food for Fireworks Night.

The Weebies Children's Daddy '**Hello Hello Hello**' was going to help '**Grumpy Gammy, Morgan the Pirate and Busy Billy**' find old wood to make the bonfire.

Each year this was a great big event in the Weebies Family calendar and where all the Weebies friends and family came together.

WEEBIES FAMILY

Alastair R Agutter

Fireworks Night

Billy Asks Grumpy Gammy What Tradition Means at Breakfast

'**Grumpy Gammy**' and '**Busy Billy**' were sitting eating their pollen pops together at breakfast time in the morning.

"Grand Dad, what is Tradition?" asked **Busy Billy**.

"Well **Billy**, it can have many meanings, but I like to think it is a time of coming together with Family and Friends to remember something special." Replied **Grumpy Gammy**.

"Our Fireworks Night is celebrating the coming of the New Year and saying farewell to the old year." Continued **Grumpy Gammy**.

"The Thing Me Bobs celebrate Fireworks Night for another reason, known as the Gunpowder Plot." Added **Grumpy Gammy**.

WEEBIES FAMILY

Alastair R Agutter

Fireworks Night

Weebies Visit the Magical Forest for Old Wood and Branches

'Hello Hello Hello, **Grumpy Gammy, Morgan the Pirate** and **Busy Billy'** flew to the **'Magical Forest'** to find some old wood and branches, to make the Bonfire they had planned.

Every year the **'Weebies Family'** would build a **'Great Big Bonfire'** to burn any old wood or rubbish they found in the Countryside left by the **'Thing Me Bobs'**.

It was a very magical time as the nights drew in and the cold of winter had finally arrived and where all the leaves had fallen from the trees.

The Weebies collected old wood, branches and rubbish all through the day from the Magical Forest and kept flying backwards and forwards to where the Bonfire was to be made, near the Weebies Family Home **'Flower Pot Cottage.'**

WEEBIES FAMILY

Alastair R Agutter

Fireworks Night

Veronica Twizzle Top, Great Aunt Andorra and Honey Cooks

Just outside **'Flower Pot Cottage'** the Weebies Family's Mummy **'Veronica Twizzle Top'** was making lots of scrumptious food, with the help of **'Great Aunt Andorra'** and **'Honey Weebie'** for the evening's celebrations.

'Great Aunt Andorra' was cutting up some pumpkins, to make a warm hearty pumpkin soup and **'Honey Weebie'** was helping by stirring the soup in the big pot as it cooked.

'Veronica Twizzle Top's' eyes were watering as she chopped up onions for the hot dogs. **'Great Aunt Andorra'** and **'Honey Weebie'** both laughed.

The Weebies were all very happy and jolly, busy talking and laughing with each other, as they made all the food for Family and Friends.

WEEBIES FAMILY

Fireworks Night

Weebies Build a Great Big Bonfire for Firework Night

Grumpy Gammy, Hello Hello Hello, Morgan the Pirate and **Busy Billy** kept flying backwards and forwards from the Magical Forest with lots of wood and old tree branches.

The Bonfire the Weebies was making got bigger and bigger, until in the end it was a **'Great Big Bonfire'** that was taller than the Weebies.

The Weebies were having lots of fun, especially **'Morgan the Pirate'** and **'Busy Billy'** for as they gathered more wood it became a game and all the time they were both laughing, for they wanted to see how big and tall they could make the Bonfire!

"Something is missing" said **Grumpy Gammy** as he admired the Great Big Bonfire! "I know we have forgotten the old Scarecrow from the lower field to put on the top" laughed **Hello Hello Hello**.

WEEBIES FAMILY

Fireworks Night

Alastair R Agutter

The Scarecrow on the Bonfire and getting the Fireworks Ready

'**Hello Hello Hello**' went down to lower field and collected the old Scarecrow and placed it on top of the Great Big Bonfire.

'**Grumpy Gammy**' started to get the Fireworks ready for the evening's fun. He made some tubes to place the rockets in, to fire up into the night's sky.

'**Morgan the Pirate**' and '**Busy Billy**' was also helping, by getting the sparklers ready.

'**Hello Hello Hello**' and '**Grumpy Gammy**' had the matches to light the Fireworks for they both knew that '**Morgan the Pirate**' was a cheeky monkey and was always up to mischief.

The evening was becoming full of magic and excitement for the Weebies Children especially.

WEEBIES FAMILY

Fireworks Night

Weebies Family Friends Arrive for Fireworks Night

It was now early evening and everyone was becoming very excited.

The Weebies Family friends began to arrive and they were all busy talking and laughing.

The Weebies Children were laughing and playing with their friends **'Nee Nee, Bethany, Shannon, Darcy, Hasty Katie and Joey Fiddly Bump.'**

'Hello Hello Hello' was passing out some sparklers to the Weebies Children and **'Grumpy Gammy'** began to light the **'Great Big Bonfire'** they had made during the day, as the sun went down.

There was a smell of cooked **'Hot Dogs'** with onions and **'Baked Potatoes'** filling the night's air and everyone was beginning to feel very hungry.

WEEBIES FAMILY

Alastair R Agutter

Fireworks Night

Time for Something to Eat for Weebies Family and Friends

As the smell of food lingered in the night's air and the **'Great Big Bonfire'** burned bright the Weebies Family and Friends all began to eat from the table hot dogs and freshly baked potatoes.

There was a lovely warm glowing heat coming from the **'Great Big Bonfire'** taking the chill off of the dark cold night.

The **'Great Big Bonfire'** crackled as the old wood and branches burned.

As always **'Morgan the Pirate'** was up to mischief and squirted lots on hot mustard onto **'Busy Billy's'** hot dog when he was not looking. His face went bright read and he coughed from tasting the very hot mustard.

WEEBIES FAMILY

Fireworks Night

Alastair R Agutter

The Fireworks Begin for the Weebies Family and Friends

The Fireworks display was about to finally begin and **'Grumpy Gammy'** was getting ready to light the first of five rockets.

All the Weebies Children were very excited with their eyes wide open in the dark of the night.

'Grumpy Gammy' carefully flew near the first Firework with his special sparkler to light the blue touch paper on the rocket.

'Hello Hello Hello' just gently reminded all the Weebies Children to stay back a safe distance to ensure none of them got hurt.

'Grumpy Gammy' finally lit the first rocket and all the Weebies Children listened to the sizzling sound of the blue touch paper a light.

WEEBIES FAMILY

Fireworks Night

26

The First Rocket Takes Off Up and Away Into the Sky

All of a sudden the first rocket took off with a loud swish flying high up into the night's sky.

The Weebies Family and Friends all cheered hurray and then they all started clapping and wishing each other a very 'Happy New Year'.

As the rocket reached further into the sky, all of a sudden the rocket made a number of large sizzling crackling sounds and then exploded in the night's sky with a sea of colourful patterns.

The Weebies Children softy spoke ooh and ah as they all stared up into the night's sky looking at the wonderful colours and patterns made by the rocket.

It was a truly magical night for the Weebies Children with cries of more Grand Dad by Morgan, Billy and Honey.

Fireworks Night

A Very Happy New Year on Weebies Fireworks Night

'Grumpy Gammy' the Children's Weebies Family Granddad lit another rocket and then another.

Soon the whole of the night's sky was full of colour from the exploding rockets.

'Busy Billy' Weebie shouted with joy "This is the best Fireworks Night ever! "

All the Weebies Family and Friends joined hands together and began to sing.

Every one of the Weebies had smiley faces as they kept singing and laughing.

The Weebies Family and Friends were all very happy as they said farewell to the old year and welcomed in the New Year.

'Honey' said "I cannot wait till next year, can you?"

WEEBIES FAMILY

Fireworks Night

Weebies Family Collection

The Weebies Family Collection of books have been specially created and designed for early learning.

Children are remarkable Human Beings and have the ability from birth to learn with great enthusiasm.

The small word why, so often asked is a question in pursuit for knowledge by your Child in this new found world.

The 21st century with all the challenges ahead for the Human Race needs the spirit and hope of knowledge to be found in every Child.

The Children of today are the custodians of Earth tomorrow. Each book is educational for a Child beginning this journey!

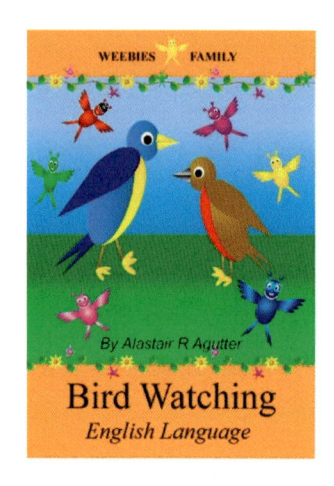

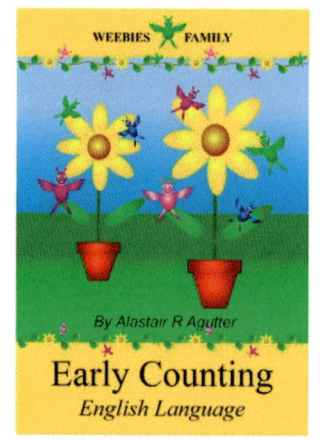

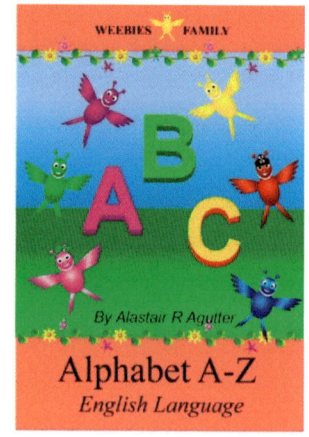

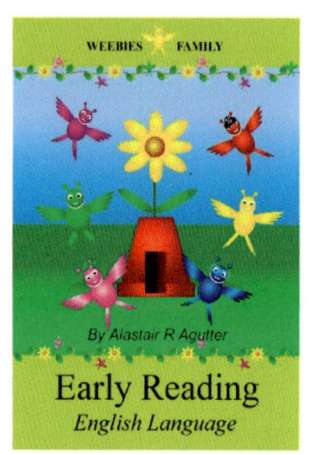

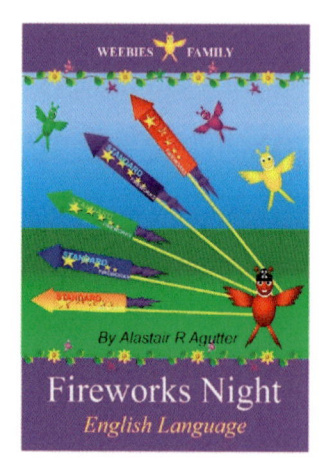

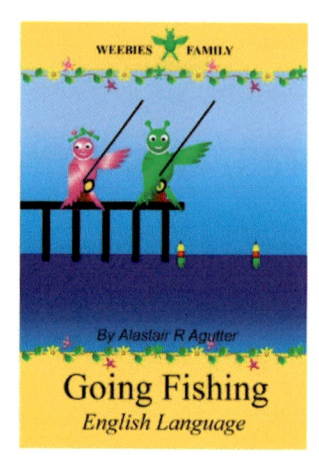

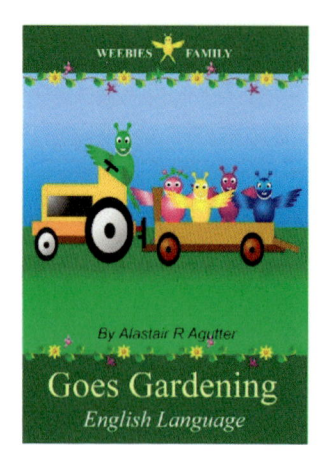

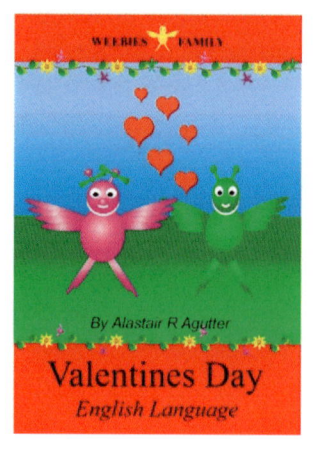

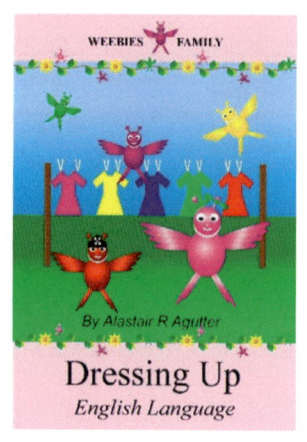

Bird Watching *English Language*	**Early Counting** *English Language*	**Alphabet A-Z** *English Language*
Early Reading *English Language*	**Fireworks Night** *English Language*	**Going Fishing** *English Language*
Goes Gardening *English Language*	**Valentines Day** *English Language*	**Dressing Up** *English Language*

The Weebies Family Complete Series and Collection of Books

Here below are details and names of each book in the Weebies Family Collection for your Children to enjoy. Thank You!

1/. Children's Weebies Family Early Reading.

2/. Children's Weebies Family Early Counting.

3/. Children's Weebies Family Dressing Up.

4/. Children's Weebies Family Alphabet A to Z.

5/. Children's Weebies Family Going Fishing.

6/. Children's Weebies Family Bird Watching.

7/. Children's Weebies Family Goes Gardening.

8/. Children's Weebies Family Valentine's Day.

The Weebies Family Complete Series and Collection of Books

9/. Children's Weebies Family Fireworks Night.

10/. Children's Weebies Family Christmas.

11/. Children's Weebies Family Spring Time.

12/. Children's Weebies Family Summer Time.

13/. Children's Weebies Family Autumn Time.

14/. Children's Weebies Family Winter Time.

15/. Children's Weebies Family at Easter.

16/. Children's Weebies Family Mother's Day.

17/. Children's Weebies Family Father's Day.

18/. Children's Weebies Family at Tea Time.

The Weebies Family Complete Series and Collection of Books

19/. Children's Weebies Family at School.

20/. Children's Weebies Family Halloween.

The Children's Weebies Family Complete Series and Collection of Books are available online and through traditional High Street Books stores internationally. Weebies Family Books are also available direct online from our printers, publishers and distributors Amazon at www.amazon.com

Please remember at the time of publishing the Amazon 'Kindle Match Program' is available to you. So when buying a Paperback through Amazon you also qualify for the Digital Kindle Book Editions Free.

The Weebies Family Books in Different Languages

All the Weebies Family Books have been published in English (British) Language. But we do plan to publish these book editions in English American, Spanish, German, Italian and French.

We will endeavour at the earliest opportunity to make sure the 'Weebies Family' of early learning books are available in most if not all languages world-wide for Children everywhere in the World to enjoy and experience that import early start in life.

Weebies books also encourage creativity in drawing, where a Child learns those very important hand co-ordination skills.

Thank You!

About The Author

Alastair R Agutter was born in Farnborough, England in 1958 to English parents.

He is a freelance (self-employed) Writer, Philosopher, Logistician, Theoretical Physicist, Author, Publisher, Naturalist, Environmentalist, Computer Scientist, Creative Digital Artist and Proud Father of Five Children.

He believes his most important job has been as a Father and is very passionate about the welfare of Children. He developed the Parental Ratings Program for the World Wide Web in 2006 to help protect minors online.

One of his favourite sayings and quotations is *"Children are not invited into this world, nor do they have a say, the least we can do is to love and care for them all"*.

He is a passionate advocate for the environment and a naturalist at heart, with a great respect for all living creatures and with founding principles for the preservation of all species, many sadly under threat today from climate change.

www.alastairagutter.com

Printed in Great Britain
by Amazon